LOOK AND FIND®

THE BATMAN

™

Illustrated by Art Mawhinney
Written by William Shears
Batman created by Bob Kane

Published by Louis Weber, C.E.O., Publications International, Ltd.
7373 North Cicero Avenue, Lincolnwood, Illinois 60712

Ground Floor, 59 Gloucester Place, London W1U 8JJ

www.pilbooks.com

www.dckids.com

8 7 6 5 4 3 2 1

ISBN 1-4127-5227-2

Deep beneath the ground under Wayne Manor lies the Batcave. Here Bruce Wayne and his butler Alfred learn of the hideous schemes that Batman's enemies are plotting. Look around for this Batgear to help equip Batman for adventures to come.

Batarang

Batman Polar Armor

Glider Wings

Batcomputer

Jet-Pack

Aquatic Outfit

Ozwald Cobblepot, a.k.a. the Penguin, has taken over the Gotham Zoo. With an army of penguins and other birds at his disposal, Cobblepot plans to wreak havoc on the city — and then the world! Find these feathered fiends before they swoop at Batman.

Cockatoo

Raven

Ostrich

Blue Jay

Eagle

Dodo

Batman's pumped-up archrival Bane is on the loose on the streets of Gotham ... and he's got destruction on his mind. Look for these bewildered bystanders and whisk them to safety.

Scotty Skittlesworth

Polly Pendleton

Ted Terry

Fred Firestein

Wally Warren

Cal Collins

DEAD END

Batman is in for a wild ride. The Joker has taken over an old amusement park. Setting a trap for our hero in this funhouse, the Clown Prince of Crime may have the last laugh. Help Batman find these scary carnival villains before it's too late!

Werewolf

Skeleton

Vampire

Bearded Lady

Clown

Strongman

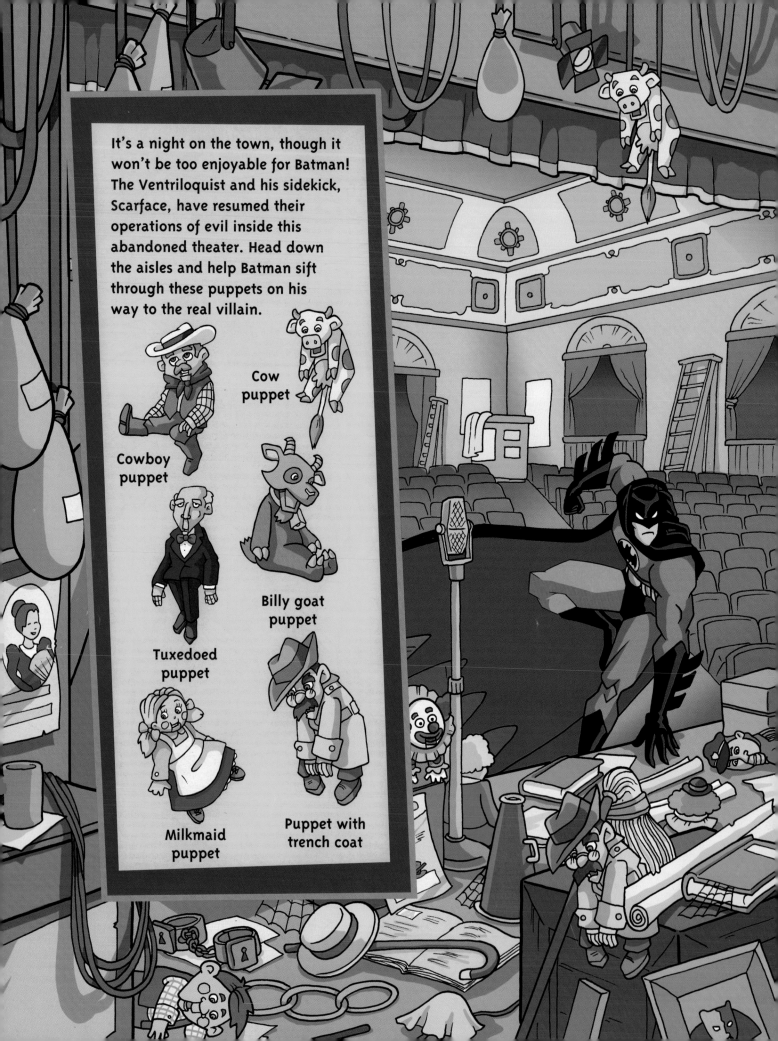

It's a night on the town, though it won't be too enjoyable for Batman! The Ventriloquist and his sidekick, Scarface, have resumed their operations of evil inside this abandoned theater. Head down the aisles and help Batman sift through these puppets on his way to the real villain.

Cow puppet

Cowboy puppet

Billy goat puppet

Tuxedoed puppet

Milkmaid puppet

Puppet with trench coat

Meow! Catwoman has slinked into a pet shop to rob it. As soon as the Dark Knight shows up to trap her, she releases the shop's animals to slow him down. Find these cats to clear the way for Batman to grab this leather-clad burglar.

Calico cat

Siamese cat

A hairless cat

A black cat

Maine Coon cat

A fluffy white cat

Wayne Enterprises is throwing its yearly Winter Charity Gala. Except this year there is an uninvited and unwelcome guest—Mr. Freeze! Find this expensive jewelry before Mr. Freeze gets his chilly claws on it.

Diamond tiara

Large blue gem necklace

Emerald-encrusted women's shoes

A large ruby ring

Gold cufflinks

A silver pocketwatch

Batman has finally locked up every villain at Arkham Asylum — where they belong. After his long battles, the Dark Knight can sleep soundly, since these ne'er-do-wells have been vanquished … or can he? Find these objects that have been smuggled past Arkham's security.

The Joker's laughing lapel flower

The Ventriloquist's dummy, Scarface

Mr. Freeze's freeze-ray gun

The Penguin's monocle

Catwoman's whip

One of Bane's thugs

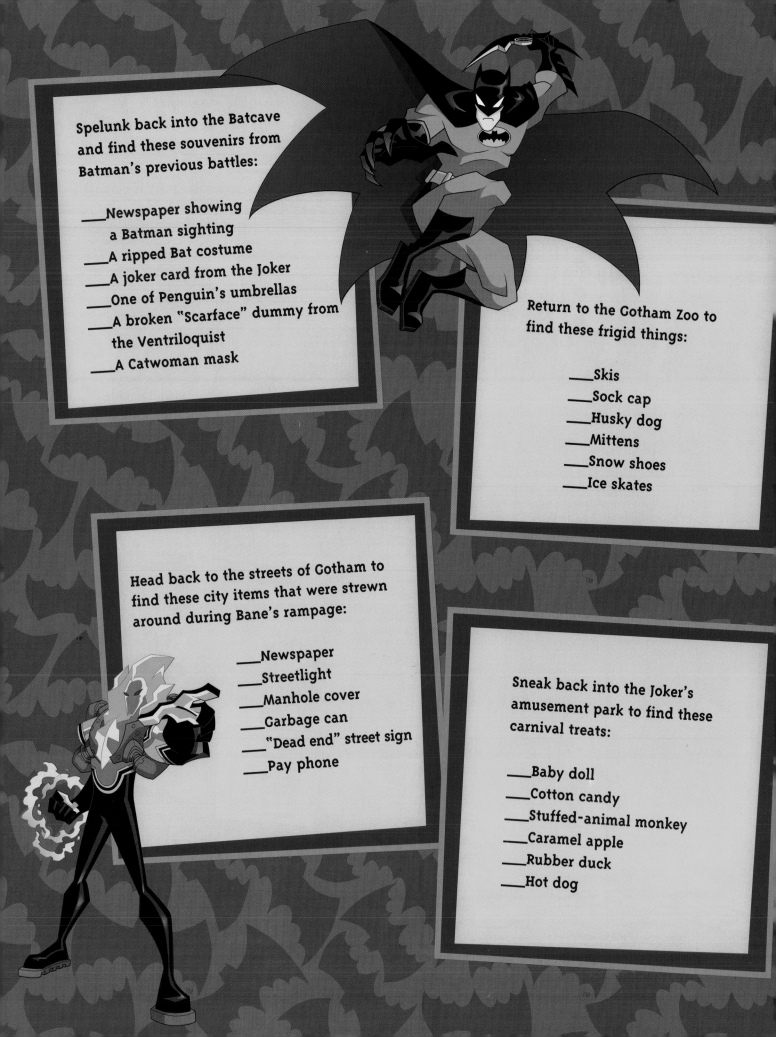

Spelunk back into the Batcave and find these souvenirs from Batman's previous battles:

___Newspaper showing a Batman sighting
___A ripped Bat costume
___A joker card from the Joker
___One of Penguin's umbrellas
___A broken "Scarface" dummy from the Ventriloquist
___A Catwoman mask

Return to the Gotham Zoo to find these frigid things:

___Skis
___Sock cap
___Husky dog
___Mittens
___Snow shoes
___Ice skates

Head back to the streets of Gotham to find these city items that were strewn around during Bane's rampage:

___Newspaper
___Streetlight
___Manhole cover
___Garbage can
___"Dead end" street sign
___Pay phone

Sneak back into the Joker's amusement park to find these carnival treats:

___Baby doll
___Cotton candy
___Stuffed-animal monkey
___Caramel apple
___Rubber duck
___Hot dog

Head through the lobby and back into the theater to give Batman a hand at finding these props that were left behind:

___Magician handcuffs
___Top hat
___Poster of a tap-dancer duo
___Ukulele
___Blonde, curly wig
___Old-fashioned microphone

Prowl back to the pet shop and look for these other feline findems:

___Cat collar
___Scratching post
___Cat litter box
___Can of cat food
___Catnip
___Toy mouse

Swing back to the Wayne Winter Charity Gala and defrost these frozen party necessities:

___Frozen champagne glass
___Frozen punch bowl
___Frozen roasted chicken
___Frozen waiter
___Frozen flower arrangement
___Frozen trumpet player

Admit yourself into Arkham Asylum to find these items:

___Straitjacket
___Handcuffs
___Syringe
___Psychiatrist
___Stretcher
___Nurse